The Ordinary Extraordinary
DOG

Who thinks he's human

By Andrew Sherriff

Lewin the dog was no ordinary dog,
he was an extraordinary dog, why was
he you might ask? Because he thought
he was human just like you and me.

Not only did he think he was human,
he thought he was a top dog. (The most
handsome, most athletic and most
intelligent dog the world had
ever seen!).

Scruffy fur
on his back

Bent tail

Smooth fur
on this side

Patches just
on this side

He slept not in a basket but in his own bed. He would cuddle up to his favourite tennis ball and have a bowl of water next to him in case he got thirsty during the night.

To wake him up in the morning his clock didn't make a ringing noise but a barking noise. He would then hop out of bed to join everyone for breakfast.

He would eat his breakfast at the table. His favourite was cornflakes but he would sometimes forget to use a spoon and go back to being a dog and stuff his nose in the bowl. His brothers thought this was hilarious because mum would go mad.

"Lewin cut that out!"

Lewin would sometimes ride to school on his scooter. It got him there super quick and gave him time to play hide and seek. He was the best at the game because he used his great sense of smell to sniff them out.

Lewin hated maths. He could only count up to two and would get so bored in class he would hold the wooden ruler in his mouth and pretend he was playing fetch the stick.

His favourite lesson was cricket because he was really good at catching the ball and would run to the stumps faster than anyone could throw!

Trouble was he always had a wee on the wickets. This drove the umpire mad but everyone else found it really funny.

On the way home, half way across the crossing Lewin would decide to have a poop. The lollipop lady would go berserk and shout

"STOP IT YOU PESKY DOG"

Even the bus driver couldn't stop himself from laughing.

Lewin just trotted off, wondering what all the fuss was about.

When Lewin got home from school he would take Oscar his pet guinea pig out for a walk. He would always end up carrying Oscar on his back because his legs are so small he couldn't keep up.

Just before bedtime Lewin liked nothing better than listening and barking along to his favourite tunes on his old record player. He thought he was singing the words in perfect tune but really he was just barking like an ordinary dog. This drove everyone nuts!

After a hard day, Lewin would fall asleep and dream of being a pirate on a desert island searching for buried treasure. He loved digging and discovering golden bones.

Goodnight!

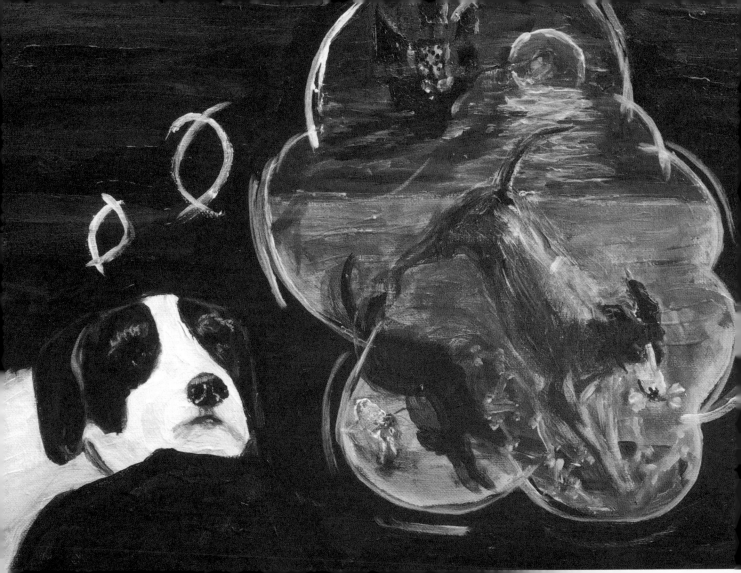

Lewin